When Tam the tortoise [...]
that what she really wa[...]
It would have to be a very *big* dog, too,
so that she could share it with her friend
Limpet. 'See if you can get one for the
price of a tortoise!' teased her father,
knowing that this was impossible.

But the impossible happened. Jill found
Brandy, who was being offered free because
he needed a home. As Jill and Limpet had
to admit, though, Brandy could only be
described as 'a dog and a half' . . . And
when Jill saw her parents' faces, her heart
sank. Would she ever be allowed to keep
him?

*Jacket illustration by Tony Morris*

# A Dog and a Half

## BARBARA WILLARD

*Illustrated by* JANE PATON

KNIGHT BOOKS
Hodder and Stoughton

Copyright © 1964 Barbara Willard
Illustrations © 1964 Jane Paton
First published in Great Britain 1964 by
Hamish Hamilton Ltd
Reprinted 1966, 1968
New edition 1977
Knight Books edition 1979

*The characters and situations in this book are
entirely imaginary and bear no relation to any real
person or actual happening*

Printed and bound in Great Britain for
Hodder and Stoughton Paperbacks, a
division of Hodder and Stoughton Ltd,
Mill Road, Dunton Green, Sevenoaks,
Kent (Editorial Office: 47 Bedford
Square, London, WC1 3DP) by
Hazell Watson & Viney Ltd,
Aylesbury, Bucks
ISBN 0 340 23776 7

# Contents

Chapter One

## *Instead of a Tortoise*

JILL and Limpet were standing in the garden on a Saturday morning in <u>spring</u>. The sun was shining cheerfully, everything was growing with great energy and vigour, the birds were singing so loudly they seemed to be shouting. But neither Jill nor Limpet felt particularly happy. They stood looking down at something they had just picked out of the big rosebed.

"Are you sure?" Jill said.

"Yes, I am sure." Limpet sighed. "Oh poor Tam!"

Jill crouched down and had another look at Tam Tortoise. There seemed little doubt about it—the hard cruel winter had killed him. In his first winter they had taken him indoors, settled him into a box filled with comfortable straw, and then found a place for the box in one of the greenhouses. But his second winter he had somehow escaped and buried himself for his long sleep, without seeking advice or help from anyone. Unfortunately the winter had been a particularly horrible one. And now here before them was the result of poor Tam's independence—there was nothing left of him but his shell.

Limpet was a year younger than Jill, but on the whole she liked him best of all her friends. This might have been partly because he was always ready to do what she suggested. It would be a bad day if Limpet suddenly dug his toes in and said *No*. His real name was Lambert Jeffreys. It was Jill's father who had nicknamed him Limpet—because there was no getting rid of him, he stuck as fast as a real limpet sticks in its shell to a rock on the seashore. Whenever Jill was at home, Limpet was there, too—it was never necessary to invite him. Apart from all other friendly reasons, he lived next door.

In this case "next door" meant on the other side of Little Paddock, a little square of ground lying between their two homes. Limpet's father kept the butcher's shop in the village, and behind his house were fields for grazing cattle. Jill's father ran a nursery garden and behind *his* house were rows and rows of greenhouses where he grew flowers for cutting, plants for gardeners, plants in pots and some grapes. And between these two lots of ground was Little Paddock, claimed by neither, useful to both, and the best playground imaginable for Jill and Limpet.

Today they went down to Little Paddock and made a hole in the ground, popped in poor Tam's shell and put a large stone to mark the place.

"Now we haven't got a tortoise," said Limpet; he always took it for granted that what belonged to Jill belonged to him, too.

She shook her head. "We haven't got a pet at all," she complained.

"Perhaps your father would buy a new tortoise."

Jill said nothing for a moment. Just then she could not help feeling that tortoises were rather unsatisfactory pets, altogether too difficult with their curious habits. You couldn't really feel very loving towards a tortoise.

"Or a dog instead of a tortoise," she said slowly. "*Would* he?"

"Have to ask," said Jill. She added thoughtfully —"It would need to be a big dog, then we could share it. I should like it to be twice as big as any other dog."

"That would be almost a pony."

"Well—once and a half times as big, then."

Presently it was half past twelve. Limpet went home to dinner. Jill went towards her own home, noticing as she went that the little yellow van with *Hyde's Nursery Ltd.* on its side was standing at the end of the drive. So her father was home.

Hoping to make a good impression, Jill hurried to brush her hair and wash her hands and arrived at the table looking so tidy that any parents would have known that something was in the air. However, in this case Jill's mother was busy ladling soup into bowls and her father was looking through a seed catalogue.

"I have a sad thing to tell, Daddy," said Jill.

"That's bad. What's happened?"

"Tam Tortoise is dead. We found his poor shell at the back of the big rosebed."

"Oh dear!" cried Jill's mother, really distressed. "I was afraid that might happen. Oh what a shame!"

"Now I haven't got a tortoise of any sort," said Jill.

Her father looked at her over the top of the seed catalogue and gave a little grin. "I don't know how many sorts there are. I suppose you'd like me to buy you a new one. That would be a different sort, wouldn't it? It would be a new tortoise instead of an old tortoise."

Jill was silent, sitting sideways on her chair and frowning.

"I was thinking of something more different than old or new," she said.

"Dear me, that sounds very complicated. You mean—not a tortoise at all? Something instead of a tortoise?"

"You are clever!" Jill cried in admiration. Sometimes she thought her father knew everything—or else he could guess what she was thinking. "Yes—I do mean that."

"I'm afraid it can't be that bicycle yet. Too much money."

"Oh *no*—not the bicycle!" Jill cried, as though that was the last thing in the world she was likely to want. "A dog."

There was a little silence and in it the word "dog" seemed to echo backwards and forwards between Jill and her parents.

"I see," said her father at last. "A dog, eh?"

"Now, Jill," her mother said, "you know how often we've talked about this, and how difficult it is. We've got all those growing things to take care of. It would be terrible if one day a whole bed of something precious got dug up because the dog wanted to bury a bone."

"But Tam buried his whole self. You never said he mustn't."

"Darling, a tortoise really doesn't take up very much room. And a tortoise is slow——you have time to stop him doing anything you don't want. But a dog. Oh dear, that's a very different story."

"A huge dog would step carefully," Jill said.

"A huge dog? Good gracious, huge dogs cost pounds and pounds to buy and to feed."

"Perhaps it wouldn't," Jill said obstinately. "You never know, there might be a huge dog just waiting and he wouldn't cost very much . . ."

"Well, you see if you can get one for the price of a tortoise!" her father cried, no doubt wanting to put an end to this conversation.

"Oh Daddy—thanks! How wonderful!"

"John, you're teasing the child. . . . He's teasing,

Jill. Now, eat up your soup before it gets stone cold and forget all about dogs and tortoises."

Jill was ready to forget about tortoises. But as she sat there she began to imagine the dog. She had been thinking about this matter for a long time, but in fact she had not known until she actually spoke of it that she wanted a large dog. It seemed to grow as she thought about it. She sat there at the table and imagined how high it would stand. Up to the table-top? Up to the dresser? She remembered seeing pictures of children in old-fashioned clothes, standing with one hand on the collar of some enormous hound. Only imagine if she could stand like that, while her mother took a coloursnap with the camera which had been her Christmas present!

"Soup, Jill!"

Jill sighed and picked up her spoon at last. She could hardly wait to tell Limpet the news. He was clever at finding things. She had not a doubt but that they would easily discover the animal of her dreams. . . .

Although it was Saturday afternoon, John Hyde did not go and sit down comfortably to read the paper. Instead, he went outside in the warm sunshine and walked through his greenhouses, inspecting this, frowning at that. By the time Jill caught up with him to ask for the promised money, he had reached the smallest of the glass houses where he kept his special treasures. There was a pot of seedlings there which, he had told Jill, might bring him fame if they turned out as he hoped.

"Come here," he called, when he saw Jill at the door. "Something to show you."

Jill went inside and her father pointed out how well his seedlings were coming along.

"They're making their second pair of leaves, look."

"What will they grow into?"

"Don't tell a soul—I hope they're going to be blue pinks."

"Goodness," said Jill. But she felt less interested than she might have done because she was thinking of other important things. "Please could you give me my tortoise money to buy the dog?"

He laughed. "Blue pinks—tortoise money for dogs ... You and I are both crazy, Jill. Here you are, then." As he handed the money over, he looked at her fondly, and added—"Look—I'm afraid this is a bit of a tease, you know. Mummy was right. You mustn't really expect to find what you want this time. And, Jill—don't be too disappointed, will you? I'd like to give you what you want, but I just can't."

"It's all right," she assured him, utterly unshaken. "I'll find it."

And she rushed away to meet Limpet, who was waiting as usual at the gate into Little Paddock. She gabbled out her news and waited for his cry of delight.

But Limpet was silent. As usual, though he was younger than Jill, he was more practical.

"There isn't enough money."

"There is—there is—there must be!"

"What about feeding it?"

"Silly, I've got my pocket money."

"Big dogs eat a lot. Big dogs eat more than just a lot."

"Well, you ought to be able to do something about that. Your father's the butcher. He must have bones and *bones*."

Limpet brightened up at this. They began to talk about the dog—its shape, size, colour, name.

"But where shall we get it?" Limpet asked.

"We'll have to take the bus into town."

"Do you know if there's a dog shop?"

"Well of course I do. There's that pet shop near the station. We'll get it there. We'll go by the two o'clock bus. I've asked Mummy."

It was not very far to the town and the bus went every hour from the crossroads. Jill and Limpet joined a number of people from the village, who were going to do a bit of week-end shopping. Before

long, they had left the bus at the station stopping-place and were rushing to the pet shop. As they went in at the door they were both feeling excited. Limpet's excitement was full of doubts, but Jill's was the happy kind that is sure things will turn out exactly right.

The shop was stacked with tins of dog food and mounds of dog biscuits in packets, with collars and leads, brushes and combs, rubber bones and balls. There were sacks of feeding stuffs for every kind of domestic animal. There were rows of empty bird-cages and a few cages with canaries and budgerigars hopping about in them. Also an aquarium full of minute tropical fish. The shop manager, wearing a brownish overall, was just unpacking a new load of goods as Jill and Limpet came in.

"Hullo, there! What can I do for you two?"

"What have you got in the way of large dogs?" asked Jill.

The manager laughed.

"Sorry, my dear. I don't keep any dogs here. Have a nice budgie and teach it to talk? Have some fish? Have a nice tortoise?"

"We've had a nice tortoise?" said Jill. "Can't you tell us where to get a dog?"

"See if there's anything on the board. People stick cards there, if they've got anything to sell. Have a look. You might find something."

As a matter of fact, Limpet was already standing in front of the board, which was covered with cards and envelopes stuck on with drawing pins and offering such things as *Two Ginger Tom Kittens,* 50p *each. Guinea-pigs: All colours. Talking Parrot and Cage. Alsatian Puppies—lovely natures, good pedigree.*

"Jill!" said Limpet. "Look!"

## Chapter Two

# *A Bus in a Garden*

"WE don't want a *donkey*, Limpet."

"Not that one, softie. This one."

He was pointing at the bottom card of all.

It said—*Good country home wanted for large dog.*

Jill half thought that someone had put it there for a joke. But who would do such a thing? Nobody. The person who had put the card on the board in the pet shop had meant every word of it.

"It doesn't say how much." Jill went back to the counter, where the shop manager was now parcelling bird seed. "Would it be a lot of money? Have they told you how much?"

"Which one's that, dear? Oh that—that big dog. I clean forgot that—it's only been on the board a couple of hours. That's Mrs. Remnant's dog. It's the good home that counts."

"Yes, but—"

"Do you mean," said Limpet in a small voice and looking quite pale with anxiety, "do you mean that it's *free*?"

"Absolutely free, gratis and for nothing," replied the man cheerfully. "A snip, that's what that is."

"He means a good bargain," Jill said to Limpet. She took an extra deep breath, afraid to get too confident in case there was some catch in the business. "Why is it free—and what you said—and for nothing?"

"Well, it's one of those sad stories, my dear. Mrs. Remnant, the owner, lives in a caravan of sorts. It's got to be moved because the ground's been bought for building. And in the place where Mrs. Remnant's going to stay they don't allow dogs."

"How awful," said Jill. "She must be miserable. Is the caravan far away?"

"It's only a step. Turn right outside the shop and keep going till you come to a high fence. There's a door in the fence and the caravan's in there."

"Thanks. Thanks very much . . . Come on, Limpet!"

They were so wild with excitement by this time that they started off to the left instead of the right. They would have gone on for miles, no doubt, if the manager of the pet shop had not seen what was happening and shouted after them.

"Why didn't you tell me we'd turned the wrong way?" Jill snapped at Limpet.

Limpet said nothing. He was used to her ways.

He put up with them because he and she were friends and because, as his father was always saying, nobody is perfect.

When at last they reached the fence they could not believe it was the right one—they had passed it scores of times and they had certainly never noticed a door. It was there, though. They stood before it and wondered whether to knock or just to open it and go inside. Jill rapped once with her knuckles, but the sound was swallowed up by the noise of the traffic in the street, and no one came to let them in. So at last they turned the handle. They pushed the door inwards, went inside, and closed the door again behind them.

It was like stepping into another world. The closed door and the high wooden fence shut off the street noises quite surprisingly. At either end of the fence there were big new blocks of flats, with blank windowless side walls which suggested that the building was not quite finished. But here, where the door was, there was just an old house fallen to pieces standing in a huge and beautiful garden. And an ancient bus with curtains at the windows.

Limpet started to stay—"Then where's the caravan—"

But Jill had already seen that the bus was the caravan—the bus was where Mrs. Remnant lived who

wanted a good country home for her dog. Inside
the bus, instead of rows of seats there must be chairs
and a table, a cooking stove and a wash basin and a
bed. Jill thought it was the most wonderful kind of
caravan she had ever seen. She stood gazing at it as
though it had laid a spell over her.

Then the front door—it was where the platform
would ordinarily be—opened slowly and a woman
wearing a flowery overall stepped out with a basin
of crusts and scraps which she threw out on to the
grass. And at once, although it was spring, birds flew
from all directions as though they knew the time and
had been waiting for this, and began to pick and

peck and fly off into the branches with the food.

The woman stood for a moment watching the birds and smiling—slightly and sadly. Then she spotted Jill and Limpet.

"Yes?" she said, and she had a rather sighing kind of voice. "Can I help you?"

Limpet gave Jill a push, so that she had to speak up.

"We saw about your dog," she said.

"My dog. . . ."

"In the pet shop. Isn't it your dog that wants a good country home?"

"A good country home," repeated the woman. And then she was silent.

Jill tried again. "Please are you Mrs. Remnant?"

The woman nodded. Even the slight smile she had given to the birds had now left her face. She took out her handkerchief, blew her nose, wiped her eyes and seemed to pull herself together.

"You'd better come inside," she said. . . .

Jill tugged at Limpet. They tried not to look too much as if they were longing to see inside the bus. When they got closer to Mrs. Remnant they saw that she would need to wipe her eyes again at any moment.

Inside the bus everything was just as Jill had expected. It was snug and neat. There were chairs and a table, just as she had thought. There was a cooking stove, a basin, a bed. But there was much more. There were pictures on the walls, lots of them. There were shelves all round covered with china ornaments. There was one small table crowded with framed photographs. There were vases of flowers, two budgerigars in a very fancy cage, an embroidered screen, cross-stitch cushions, several calendars with colour-photographs of dogs and flowers, a rocking-chair painted red, piles of books and magazines, and an ancient gramophone with a green and yellow horn like an enormous ear-trumpet.

And in the midst of all this, sitting on a round home-made rug, was an enormous white dog. His hair was slightly curly and he had a number of red-brown patches. His eyes were small and sad—indeed his expression was very much like Mrs. Remnant's.

"Is that—?" began Jill.

Mrs. Remnant nodded.

"He's a St. Bernard, isn't he?" said Limpet. "I've got a picture in a dog book."

Mrs. Remnant nodded. "A St. Bernard—yes. His name's Brandy. He's eight years old and he's the best friend I have in all the world. But they're turning me out of here and so we've got to be parted. I'm going to live with my nephew and his wife and *she* won't have him. What can I do? I've tried to find

somewhere, but he needs exercise. And I can't afford
to buy a house with a garden."

Jill went and stood by Brandy. She put her hand
on his collar. He turned his head very slightly
towards her. Then he shifted his position and with a
sigh he leant against her. She staggered slightly.
Goodness. He was a weight!

"Oh Brandy," murmured Jill. "Limpet—speak
to him."

Limpet went and stood on the other side of
Brandy. He was not much taller than Brandy, even
though the dog was sitting down.

"Much better than a tortoise, Jill." He put his
arms round Brandy's neck, and they both sighed.

"You'll never believe the trouble I've had, one
way and another," said Mrs. Remnant. "Well, I'll
put the kettle on. We'll have a cup of tea and then I'll
tell you all about it."

Certainly it was a very sad tale that Mrs. Remnant
related to Jill and Limpet. They sat round the table
drinking tea out of pink cups with gold rims. In the
middle of the table was a plate with a silver handle
and a wonderful collection of cream biscuits, which
turned out to be rather soft.

"I lived here with my dear husband," Mrs. Remnant said. "The whole place belonged to a cousin
who went years ago to New Zealand. That's why

the builders haven't been able to get the land—they couldn't find the owner, he seems to have completely disappeared—we haven't heard for years—just gone on living here. But now there's been a law suit and they've let the builders have the land for another block of flats. So I've got to go."

Unfortunately, the bus was so old and rickety, for all its cosiness, that it was hopeless to think of moving it. Anyway, where could it go? A bus with curtains and a chimney stack is not an easy thing to place.

"Worst of all is the garden," said Mrs. Remnant. "It'll just be swept away along with the ruins of the old house. I've worked on that garden for years and years. It's a picture when summer comes. I've got a little greenhouse, too. When I was a girl I worked with plants and it's hard to stop. My father had a big nursery garden not far away from here."

"That's like my father!" cried Jill. "He's Mr. John Hyde of Hyde's Nursery. It's a wonderful place. And he's got a special greenhouse where he grows secret things."

"Then mind he keeps it secret," advised Mrs. Remnant. "You can't be too careful." She blew her nose yet again, and dabbed at her eyes. "We ought to get things settled, I suppose," she said. "Have you really come to offer Brandy a home?"

"He's exactly what we're looking for, Mrs. Remnant."

"And it's all right with your parents? It's not just an idea of your own?"

"Oh *no*! He's instead of a tortoise."

"He's just the dog for you," she said. "He's used to gardens, you see. Your father's the man to appreciate such a dog. Brandy would never dig or scratch or anything like that. And he's so gentle. And he's so quiet. He used to bark a lot and when the flats were built people started to complain. So I taught him to bark in a whisper and he'd never think of barking any other way now."

"You could always come and visit him," Jill said. "We shall love him hugely because he is huge and needs it. If it's all right with you—we could take him now."

At that Mrs. Remnant gave a wail and put both hands over her eyes.

"Take him!" she cried. "No—wait! I must give him a last hug. If only I could explain—but perhaps he doesn't need it. He's so intelligent. Now—now go! I don't want to look! Take him!"

For a moment Jill wondered if Brandy would have ideas of his own about all this. But perhaps he really did understand what was happening, for he moved after them at once, out of the bus and down the steps, across the garden and through the door in the fence. Just once, as the door was opened, he paused and turned his head. Then as though deciding there was nothing for it, he lumbered through the door and stood waiting while Limpet closed it carefully.

The three of them moved off together down the main road, heading for home. In spite of the fact that Mrs. Remnant's distress had taken some of the excitement out of the business, Jill's heart thumped with pleasure to realise that this splendid great dog was hers.

"Let's walk back over the downs," she said. "I'm sure he'd like a run. Oh Limpet—I can hardly wait to see their faces when we get home!"

# Chapter Three

## *A Good Country Home*

IT took about an hour to walk home over the downs instead of going by bus. They would be back rather later, of course, but Jill said no one would mind that —they would be much too delighted with Brandy to utter one word of reproach.

"They don't know what's in store for them, Limpet."

When Jill wanted a thing really badly she always felt positive that everything about it was right. There had been times when she discovered too late that the whole thing had been a mistake. Obviously, nothing of that kind could happen over the matter of Brandy.

The spring day was nearly over. Above the smooth rolling downs the sky was clear and the air smelt good. They would walk up here often with Brandy, Jill thought. Their lives would be altogether changed by his arrival, and things that had amused them till now were sure to seem less exciting. They would do everything to make Brandy happy. How soon would he forget Mrs. Remnant? Or perhaps, since forgetting her would be a rather cruel thing to do, he might come to remember her fondly as the person who had found him his good country home.

"He likes it on the downs!" Jill cried.

She began to leap and run. Limpet rushed after her, shouting. And Brandy ran, too, strongly stretching himself in great long bounds, easily leaving them behind.

"He wouldn't run away, would he?" Limpet said uneasily.

"Of course he wouldn't. There—he's stopping now. You can see he knows where he belongs. He's yours, too, Limpet," Jill said, filled with a feeling of wonderful good temper and generosity. "So you'll ask your father about bones, won't you?"

Limpet nodded. "I shan't want to go to school on Monday morning, will you?" he said. "Jill—"

"What is it?"

"Where will Brandy sleep?"

Jill had not thought about this, but the moment she did so there seemed only one obvious answer.

"At the foot of my bed."

Limpet looked at her. He opened his mouth—then closed it again without speaking. They went on a little way in silence, then he said—

"Will he sleep at the foot of my bed, too?"

"Oh *no*. Of course not."

"You did say he was mine as well."

"I know I did. So he is. I'll look after where he's to sleep, and you look after what he's to eat."

"H'm," said Limpet.

Soon they had reached the end of the track over the downs. Below them was the village, like a toy arranged on the floor. There was all the shining glass of Hyde's Nursery, and there the fields belonging to Limpet's father, Mr. Jeffreys the butcher. There was Little Paddock, between the two properties, with a gate into each.

Jill and Limpet, with Brandy obligingly bounding behind them, started down the long slope in the direction of home.

Somehow this last half mile or so of the way home went almost too quickly. Of course Jill was longing to show Brandy to her mother and father—she kept saying so. She said again and again how delighted they were going to be, how wonderful it was for all of them that this thing had happened. Even so, she found herself hanging back a bit, walking more and more slowly. She found herself looking at Brandy with an almost frightened feeling.

"Limpet—he seems to have grown on the way home."

"He couldn't," said Limpet reasonably.

"I know he couldn't really. All the same," Jill insisted, "I didn't think he was quite so big. Do you think he's too big after all?"

"Too big for what?"

"Well—too big for a dog."

"How can he be? He can't change his size. And nor can you. You can't cut off his head and his tail."

"How silly you are!" cried Jill in a snappish manner. "Sometimes you really are a stupid sort of boy. . . . Where are you going?"

"Home."

"There you are, you see. You *are* stupid. You can't just go off home. I've got to show Brandy to Mummy and Daddy. Don't you want to show him to them, too? After all, he's half yours."

Limpet stuck out his lower lip and scowled. For a moment it seemed as though he might be going to sulk. But he was so used to doing what Jill wanted, that he soon changed his mind and followed her past his own door to hers.

When Jill and Limpet, with Brandy between them, walked in at the gates of Hyde's Nursery and went towards the house, John Hyde was standing in the drive bending over the open bonnet of the little yellow van.

"Shall we surprise him or what?" Jill asked in a panicky whisper.

With every second she became more aware of the possible mistake she had made. There was going to be trouble—she was sure of it now that she was home and saw all the everyday things that had seemed so unimportant while she was with Mrs. Remnant. In her heart she had known her father was teasing about the tortoise money. But she had obstinately refused to believe she could not get what she wanted. She had called Limpet stupid, but she was the stupid one. And now what was she going to do?

"Daddy!" she called.

"Hullo, there!" he called back, without taking his head from among the bits of engine he was inspecting so carefully.

"Daddy—*look*!"

He lifted his head just briefly, as though he would look and smile and get back to his job. Then he paused and stared. Then he straightened himself rather slowly and carefully. He shut the bonnet of the car and saw that the catch was firm—all without speaking. Then he left the van and came towards where the three of them were standing, wiping his hands on an oily rag as he came, saying "Well!" and looking not angry, certainly not excited, but absolutely stunned.

"He's Brandy, Daddy."

"He's what?"

"His name's Brandy."

"Is it, though."

"He didn't cost anything at all—not even the tortoise money, so I can give it back to you."

"No. You keep it."

"He's lovely, isn't he?" Jill cried.

Her father looked at Brandy for a long time. Then he nodded.

"Yes," he agreed. "He's lovely. A beautiful dog. He's also an enormous, hungry and quite impossible pet. Jill—we'd better get this over right away, I'm sorry, my darling. He'll have to go back."

Jill looked at her feet.

"Part of him's mine, Mr. Hyde," said Limpet.

"Does your father know that?"

Limpet shook his head.

"You'd better get off home, old boy," said John Hyde.

Limpet looked miserably at Jill.

"Goodnight, then, Jill."

"Goodnight," she said, clearing her throat first. Limpet flung his arms round Brandy's neck.

"Goodnight—I mean, good-bye, Brandy."

"Oh *lord*!" Jill's father sounded quite desperate. "I should have known better. Jill—"

"Yes, Daddy?" She sounded like Mrs. Remnant when she had put both hands over her eyes.

"Look—let's try to be sensible. I was a stupid old fool to tease you as I did. It never occurred to me for one moment . . . Well, don't you see—the very fact that I said you must get your dog for the price of a tortoise was the same as saying you wouldn't be able to have it. And now look. . . . Where in the world did you find him?"

"He was in an advertisement. . . . Free. . . . I don't know what Mrs. Remnant's going to say. I don't know how she~~'ll bear~~ it if I take him back. She's nowhere to take him—they're turning her out—"

At this moment Jill's mother came out of the house.

"This is Brandy, Margaret," her husband said, pulling a long face. "We're in terrible trouble, my dear."

"Yes, I can see you are. Of course he's a wonderful dog—really wonderful." She put her arms round Jill and gave her a very loving hug. "Don't, Jill.

Stop crying. We all make mistakes. Daddy made one, too. You and he will just have to forgive one another. Because I don't think you can put all the blame on him. I <u>think</u> you must have known, really, what he meant about the tortoise money. Didn't you?"

"I knew it too quietly," Jill wept. "I just couldn't hear it."

All this time Brandy was standing, panting slightly, his sad eyes shifting from Jill to her parents and back to Jill again. Then without any warning he sat down, settling his weight gently on the gravel drive, lifted his splendid head and gave a very soft, short howl.

"Heavens!" said Margaret Hyde. "How quiet."

"He barks in a whisper," Jill said.

"He *what*?"

"She taught him. Mrs. Remnant taught him. Because of the neighbours. Oh you don't know how clever he is. And used to gardens. Never digs or scratches, she says. Oh Brandy . . . Oh dear . . ."

"Mrs. who did you say?" asked her father. "Mrs. Remnant? I think I'll have to go and ring her up, Jill."

"She's not on the telephone."

"Are you sure?"

"How can she be? She lives in a bus."

To her astonishment, because by this time Jill could hardly believe that life would ever go right for her again, her father suddenly began to laugh.

"I must say you don't do anything by halves, do you, Jill? Barks in a whisper—lives in a bus. . . ."

"It isn't Mrs. Remnant who barks in a whisper."

"And it isn't Brandy who lives in a bus . . ."

"Well, yes . . . Well, no . . . Well, he used to. . . ."

"John," his wife said, with a quick sharp sound in her voice that told them she had come to some decision, "let's talk about it in the morning."

"You mean he can stay? Mummy. . . ."

"Till the morning. I really don't see what else is to be done." Her mother looked at Jill and she, too, was laughing. "Really, it's all too *absurd* . . . Look, Jill—dry your eyes and blow your nose—"

"Like Mrs. Remnant?"

"Never mind Mrs. Remnant now. Run round quickly to Mr. Jeffreys and ask if he can find you a good parcel of meat scraps for Brandy's supper."

## Chapter Four

## *Member of the Household*

WHEN morning came Jill sprang from her bed and dragged on her clothes as fast as possible. Then she rushed downstairs.

Brandy had not been allowed to sleep at the foot of her bed, which was disappointing. Instead he had been given a comfortable place in the kitchen, with two old blankets laid on great quantities of newspaper.

It was early and no one was about. Jill opened the kitchen door carefully, half afraid that Brandy might have been a dream dog and would by now have vanished. But his nose was already pushed against the door and he was blowing softly as she turned the handle.

There he stood, his tongue lolling out and his tail —it seemed yards from his face—gently waving. Truly he was enormous. The whole kitchen looked half its size because of him. He was as big as a table or an armchair. He was wonderful.

"Come on," whispered Jill. "We're going out."

She opened the outside door and Brandy pushed

ahead of her and bounded up the gravel drive. Jill rushed off towards Little Paddock, and he followed. She heard his great feet padding behind her, and sometimes the little click of his nails against a stone. She wondered how she had managed without a dog all these years.

Brandy particularly liked Little Paddock. He seemed to measure it with his nose and she could tell he approved because of the way he grinned as he lolloped about—even his sad little eyes, with their drooping lids, looked quite cheerful and happy. He rushed from point to point, making Little Paddock his own.

Suddenly Limpet was sitting on the gate watching. Jill had not seen him come from his house and run down the path, but she might have known that if she had woken up early, then he would have done so, too.

"He's real, then," said Limpet.

"Of course he's real!" Jill cried, quite forgetting her own waking thought that he might never have existed outside imagination. "He's wonderfully and hugely real!"

"But what's going to happen next?" asked practical Limpet. "My father says you'll never be able to keep him."

"It's what *my* father says that counts."

"That's what he meant," Limpet replied.

"Pooh!" cried Jill, unable to think of anything else convincing to say. She picked up a stick and hurled it across Little Paddock, and Brandy went after it to please her. He picked it up and broke it instantly into five pieces.

Presently it was time for breakfast. Limpet went out of his gate, Jill went out of hers with Brandy behind her. Little Paddock was left solitary between the two homes.

"There you are," said her mother, as Jill ran into the house. She gave her daughter a rather doubtful smile and glanced at Brandy. "He's still here, then?"

Jill opened her mouth to reply but her father came into the room before she could speak. When he saw Brandy he stood still and looked at him in silence.

"Ah," he said at last.

"Did you think it was all a dream, Daddy?"

"Perhaps I did."

"So did Mummy. She didn't say so but she looked so. But it wasn't all a dream—don't worry. He really is here. Look at him. Brandy. Isn't he wonderful?"

They all three stood there, looking at Brandy and thinking very different thoughts. At last all these stares made him nervous. His tail stopped waving and hung down between his legs. He dipped his great head and gave them all a miserable, sidelong glance from his sad eyes. Then very slowly and quietly he moved off to his corner and sat with his back <u>turned</u>.

" He thinks you don't want him ! " cried Jill. And she rushed to him, and hurled herself down beside

him, clasping him round the neck and telling him he was the most wonderful dog in the world—and the cleverest—and the biggest. . . .

" Come and have breakfast," said her mother. She looked very quickly at her husband, and said— " Perhaps you could make him some sort of kennel, John. . . . Porridge or cornflakes? "

" Cornflakes. . . . Kennel? He needs a whole shed."

" Well, there's the little shed next to the garage— it only needs <u>repairing</u>."

" H'm," he said. " Sugar, please, Margaret. Jill— leave that dog alone and come and get your breakfast. You'll be late for church."

" Here," said her mother, putting some cornflakes and milk into a pie dish, " give him this. I'll get him some proper dog biscuits tomorrow when I go to the village."

Jill gave Brandy the dish then quickly took her place at the table. She said nothing about the kennel, nothing about the dog biscuits. Limpet was waiting for her when she ran off to church. He looked at her but did not ask any questions, and Jill did not tell him what she knew he wanted to hear. She somehow felt she dared not speak of it. She walked very quickly with Limpet tagging along behind her. Various other boys and girls were on their way. Most of them were school friends and when Jill saw them she stopped so suddenly that Limpet ran into her.

"Don't tell anyone," she commanded.

Limpet looked dreadfully disappointed. Although his father had made him certain they would have to lose Brandy, he wanted at least to have a bit of fun talking about him. But Limpet was used to doing as Jill said. So he followed her up the little winding path into the village church, sad and silent.

Miss Todd, who played the organ, had a way of making hymns sound gay and rollicking, and everyone sang at the top of his voice. But though they sang, too, it had to be admitted that Jill and Limpet did so in a rather distracted way. What was happening at home? About the kennel—about repairing the shed? Suppose Mrs. Remnant had had second thoughts, and was even now telephoning Hyde's Nursery to ask if she could have Brandy back? Suppose Jill's mother was saying thankfully *Please come and fetch him*?

When the time came to go home, Jill pushed and shouldered her way out, in a manner that caused some grown-ups, arriving for the next service, to exclaim in disapproval. But Jill rushed on, and soon Limpet was running beside her.

"Come on home and see him," she shouted over her shoulder.

"If he's still there," he shouted back.

Perhaps if it had been Limpet who had taken Brandy home things might have been different—his father was rather stiff and stern at times, and his mother was a very small, quiet woman who seldom spoke. Jill was certain she could rely on her parents —she was certain but she ran all the faster, remembering that uncomfortable thought she had had about Mrs. Remnant changing her mind. Suppose, just this most important once, her parents, too, had decided to be stern.

Jill reached her own gate, swung in, and breathless by now, pelted up the drive towards the house.

As she did so, she saw Brandy sitting outside the front door. He had the appearance of being on guard. He looked—surely—as though he knew the house was his house. When he saw Jill he rose at once, gave his polite bark, stretched, and came lumbering to meet her.

At the same instant, her mother came out of the house.

"Your friend Mrs. Remnant telephoned."

"Mummy . . . ?" For a second Jill wondered if she would have to stop breathing altogether.

"She wanted to know if Brandy had settled down."

"Did you . . . ? What did you . . . ?"

"I told her it was too soon to say."

Jill's breath returned. They might not have decided absolutely for Brandy—but at least they had not decided entirely against.

A dog makes a great difference to the affairs of a household. At first he is like an important guest and everyone watches to see what he will do next. Then he becomes a whole new member of the family. That was how it happened with Brandy. The days went by and nothing more was said about his returning to Mrs. Remnant.

The shed was repaired and became Brandy's shed. A bale of straw was brought up from the store and spread to make a good bed for Brandy. Every evening after his father closed the shop, Limpet came running with a parcel of meat and bones and leftovers. There was a large bag of dog biscuits in the larder. A dog-brush and a steel comb had appeared and been given a place on the shelf in the scullery. Behind the kitchen door there was a special hook where Brandy's lead hung. Someone had to remember to re-fill his drinking bowl at least twice a day. And when John Hyde went one day on business to London, he returned with a splendid new collar— a beautiful wide collar, smelling splendidly of new leather, and trimmed with brass studs.

"Oh if only—" Jill began, when she saw Brandy wearing his new collar. Then she stopped. She had been going to say *If only Mrs. Remnant could see him now*! But she really did not care much to think about Mrs. Remnant, left all alone, and no doubt by this time busy about the dreaded task of clearing out the bus, packing, going away to a place she did not like . . .

Brandy meanwhile behaved as only a dream dog can. He did not dig holes, or scratch up plants, or make any mess or any noise. He barked his soft bark and did as he was told, even to fetching the shopping basket and his dinner dish, which he would drop with a clatter on the scullery floor. Everybody liked him; old Mr. Jackson, who worked at the nursery, and Mary his niece, who helped him in the afternoons—and all the others except one new man John Hyde had recently taken on. His name was Donald. There seemed absolutely no reason why Brandy should have taken a dislike to him. Except that Jill and Limpet did not care for him very much, either.

Some people thought it madness for the Hyde family to have taken on such a large dog. There was Auntie Katie, for instance. She was always a disapproving person. She would telephone and disapprove so loudly that her voice at the other end of the wire, rather like some kind of giant duck, could be heard almost all over the house.

"However are you managing?" Jill heard Auntie Katie quacking one day. "That enormous creature! You must be crazy, Margaret! A St. Bernard, too. St. Bernards are meant to live in the mountains and rescue people buried in the snow."

"There aren't any mountains here, Katie, or I'm sure Brandy would make a wonderful rescuer."

"You'll wear yourself out, Margaret! Those great feet treading mud all over the house! That long coat moulting all over the furniture! You've got enough to do as it is!"

Margaret looked at Jill and laughed silently. Auntie Katie was making so much noise that it hurt —it became necessary to hold the telephone receiver quite a long way away.

"I'm afraid poor Katie just doesn't understand about dogs, Jill," her mother said, when the conversation at last came to an end. . . . "Fetch the brush and comb for me. I've just got time to give Brandy a grooming."

Brandy stood patiently to be brushed and combed. Once the comb caught in a tangle and gave him a terrible tug. He swung round almost as though he was going to bite. Then at once he wagged his tail and pushed his head against Margaret's hand, as though apologising for forgetting his manners.

"He's really wonderful, Jill," her mother said, looking at Brandy with pride. "What a lovely coat! There—put his collar on again—the new one. Daddy's going to take him for a run on the downs."

"I'll call Limpet, then we can go, too."

"Not this time, darling. Daddy wants to have a really fast walk. You'll never keep up and he doesn't want to be hindered."

Jill went down to the gate and watched her father and Brandy go striding up the lane to the downs. She leant against the gatepost even after they were out of sight. As she stood there, Limpet arrived with the evening parcel for Brandy.

"What's up?" asked Limpet.

"Nothing."

"You look cross."

"I'm only thinking," said Jill. But she would not tell him what.

She was in fact considering the matter of her parents' interest in Brandy. Her mother groomed him, her father exercised him. You might almost think he had been their idea from the start. It would have been very stupid of Jill to complain about this, for it meant that Brandy had indeed become a member of the household—just one of the Hyde family, belonging to no one more than another.

Jill and Limpet took the parcel of meat into the kitchen. They cut it up and mixed it with some good hard biscuit. They filled his bowl with clean water and then went to the shed and plumped up his bed, putting down some fresh straw—he was so heavy that he soon trampled it almost to dust and it was always being renewed.

"Here they come!" cried Limpet, as he and Jill turned away from the shed.

John Hyde was striding up the drive with Brandy at his heels. Most surprisingly, Brandy was being led.

Jill rushed outside.

"Oh why is his lead on? He didn't bite someone? He wasn't in a fight? He didn't chase the sheep?"

"No fighting, no biting," her father replied. He sounded cheerful enough. Indeed, he burst out laughing as he added—"It was just that he tried to get on the five-thirty bus at the crossroads."

## Chapter Five

# *Why?*

THE idea of a dog trying to catch a bus seemed extremely funny to Jill's family. Jill, too, did her best to treat it as a huge joke.

"But you would have no money for your fare!" she cried, clasping him round the neck.

"And where would he sit?" said her mother.

"He'd have to go on the top deck," decided her father. "Do you think he'd ever get up the stairs?"

Brandy sat with his tongue hanging out, looking, it was decided, rather foolish.

In the middle of the night, Jill surprisingly found herself wide awake. Without meaning to, she began to think. Of course she thought about Brandy. First she thought of him in a loving way—of how wonderful it was to have him living with them—of how good and funny he was. And even if her parents did sometimes behave rather as if he was *theirs*, how much better this was than their first impulse—which had been to pack him off home instantly to Mrs. Remnant.

And then all these comfortable thoughts vanished.

Something which had been kept at the very back of Jill's mind ever since Brandy and her father returned from their walk now would no longer be ignored. This uneasy something was in the shape of a question.

*Why* had Brandy tried to catch the bus?

Jill rolled over in bed and hid her face in the pillow. But though this very nearly stopped her breathing, it could not stop her thinking. There seemed to be only one answer to the question. But because she did not want it to be the right one, Jill quickly invented others. Perhaps he had done it to tease her father—or to frighten the bus conductor—or just as one of his lumbering jokes. For he did play tricks on them, often. He would take away a glove or a shoe and crouch over it while everyone ran round frantically searching. Then, just as they were giving up in despair, he would leap across the room with the glove or the shoe dangling in his mouth, and he would shake it in a teasing way and growl when they tried to take it from him. He seemed sometimes to be doing it out of kindness, as though he felt they enjoyed being amused and that he owed them something for his board and lodging.

And so, Jill thought obstinately, he might very well have been having one of these playful fits when he tried to get on the bus. . . .

She sighed. Beyond her window the night was quite light, for there was a full moon sailing across the top of the sky. Jill slid out of bed and found her slippers and dressing gown. Then she crept downstairs and let herself out by the kitchen door. Very quietly, she walked along the grass edge of the path until she reached the shed by the garage, which was Brandy's kennel.

The shed had a door like a stable. The night was quite warm so the top half of the door was wide open. Perhaps Brandy had heard Jill coming, in spite of her care in walking on the grass. For he did not bark, just stood up in the straw and swung his tail. The moonlight shone into the shed and made his eyes glitter like red glass.

Jill slid back the bolt and went inside.

"Why?" she asked. "Oh why, why did you try to get on the bus?"

He sighed, leaning against her. But then he often sighed, so it told her nothing. She rumpled up the straw for him, hugged him and smoothed his lovely coat, then went out once more. She leant over the door and saw that he had settled down comfortably. She thought he looked more cheerful.

"It was because you wanted to tease Daddy," she told him firmly.

Then she went away quickly and hurried into bed

and stopped thinking, because she instantly fell asleep.

Next morning, Limpet joined Jill as usual on the way to school.

"What about Brandy, Jill?"

"Well—what about him?"

"I mean the bus," said Limpet solemnly.

"Oh that. What about that?" Jill repeated in an irritating way.

"Why? Why did he do it? That's what I want to know."

"Because he was playing a joke on Daddy, of course. Why else?"

Limpet did not reply.

"He often plays jokes, Limpet—you know that."

Limpet looked at her and then as quickly looked away.

"My father knows why he did it."

Jill thought privately that Limpet's father always seemed to know more than anybody else, but she could not say so.

"How can he?" she said coldly. "He wasn't there."

Limpet shrugged. Jill scowled. They were very near to quarrelling. They walked on in silence, but as they parted at the school gates Limpet looked over his shoulder and shouted out—

"He's homesick!"

Jill almost burst into tears, but there was no time —school was just starting. She almost hated Limpet for saying out loud what she had so carefully tried to hide from herself. How could Brandy possibly be homesick? They did everything for him. They had given him a beautiful kennel, and they fed him huge meals that he always enjoyed. They took him for long walks and they loved him. What could any dog alive want more than all that? He *must* like it better than living in a bus.

Jill had a bad day. She could not do her lessons and she got into serious trouble for talking and behaving in a noisy, stupid fashion. When the day ended at last she rushed away home without waiting for Limpet, even though she heard him call after her in a furious, wailing kind of voice.

Jill dashed into the kitchen where her mother was baking cakes.

" Where's Brandy? Where is he? "

" He's in his kennel. "

" In his kennel? Now? What for? Why is he in his kennel? It's nearly his dinner time. "

" Jill! What's the matter with you? Don't talk to me like that. Behave yourself. You and Brandy both seem to be in a bad mood. "

" Brandy's *never* in a bad mood. . . . " Then Jill's voice trailed away, for she saw by her mother's expression that something had gone wrong. " Mummy . . . ? "

" He's dug a great hole in the new grass by the gate, " her mother said.

" But he never digs holes— "

" Jill! Don't stand their saying he never does this

and he never does that. He has done it. He's dug a great hole in the new grass. Go and look, if you like. He's in disgrace. Daddy's furious, and I don't wonder at it."

Jill rushed outside. She knew what she would see but she had to see it before she could be positive the whole thing was not some unpleasant kind of dream. There was the hole all right. It was huge. You might suppose Brandy had set about burying his whole enormous self, not just a bone from last night's meal.

As she stood there staring at the horrible mess, at the young green grass scattered far and wide and the great gaping dark hole, Jill knew that Limpet had arrived with today's food parcel and was standing watching her.

"Come here and look at this, Limpet."

He moved inside the gate and came to stand beside her.

"Better stop giving him bones, Jill—do you think?"

"What good would that do?"

"If he hasn't got any bones, he can't bury them."

Jill was remembering remarks made by grown-ups when she herself had from time to time done senseless, destructive things for no apparent reason. There was the time she turned a jar of flowers upside down on the dining-room table when Auntie Katie had come to lunch. Jill heard the grown-up words that had greeted this incident—and she heard them, not in her memory, but coming out of her own mouth as she stood with Limpet looking at the dreadful hole.

"He's trying to draw attention to himself," she said.

Limpet was silent. Jill turned to look at him. One large tear was running down the left side of his face. He caught it with his tongue and sniffed furiously.

"What are we going to do, Jilly?"

"Ought we to . . . ? Oh—I don't know."

"We ought to go and see Mrs. Remnant."

"She'll be gone by now."

"She might not. She wasn't sure when, was she?"

"Perhaps it'll be all right. Perhaps this is the only thing he'll do," Jill said.

She and Limpet seemed to have stopped quarrelling. . . .

For two or three days, all went well. Brandy was forgiven, the hole was filled up and no more was said. He was quiet and well-behaved and sighed a lot.

But on a fine Sunday he went to sleep stretched across several boxes full of seedling pansies and flattened every one. And two days after that he took a cushion from the sitting-room and tore it to shreds. Three days after that he knocked over a pile of fifty new flower-pots and broke the lot.

"I wonder he doesn't go right into the greenhouses and tear things up there!" John Hyde said furiously. "Just let him, that's all. I can tell you one thing, I'm locking up my experimental seedlings from now on. Or do you think he'll simply tear the door down?"

For the seedlings of the pink that was intended to be blue had flourished in the increasingly fine weather. They had become neat little plants and two small buds had appeared. One day, those buds would open and show their colour at last.

"And another thing, Jill," her father said, and he was really angry or he would never have made it sound as though it was all her fault, "he keeps on snarling at Donald. That young man's the best worker I've had—and he knows just about everything there is to know about horticulture. I'm not going to have him leaving simply because we've got an uncontrollable dog."

Both Jill and Limpet now felt they must go in search of Mrs. Remnant. Although Limpet was sure she would have gone by now, Jill was just as sure they could find out where she had gone. The man in the pet shop might know.

They got on the bus and went to the town, and they walked towards the fence behind which Mrs. Remnant had been living when they first met her. But they found everything changed. The high fence had been pulled down, a bulldozer was inside tearing up the garden, the remains of the old house had vanished. And so, completely, had the bus in which Mrs. Remnant and Brandy had had their home.

"Told you," said Limpet.

Jill did not answer, but turned at once for the pet shop.

The man behind the counter looked at them over his glasses.

"Hullo. Seen you two before, haven't I? What can I do for you today? How about a nice tortoise?"

"We've been looking for Mrs. Remnant," Jill said.

"Left here two weeks back, Mrs. Remnant did, poor old soul. There's her budgies—over there. I'm looking after them for her—she's only a couple of miles away. It's her niece is the trouble. Very fussy about the house. Won't have dogs, doesn't like budgies."

"Please will you tell us her address?" Jill said. "We've got her dog Brandy. We—well, we thought she might like to know how he's getting on."

"That's right, dear," said the man. "Send her a little note—she'll like that. And if she comes in about the birds I'll tell her you were in. Here—I'll write the address on this bit of paper. Dog doing nicely, is he?"

"We think he's the most wonderful dog in the world," Jill said truthfully.

"Ah—I always called him a dog and a half, my-self," said the man, smiling to remember Brandy. "A dog and a half, that's what he is."

Jill and Limpet took the piece of paper with Mrs. Remnant's address and said good-bye. On the way home in the bus they discussed what they should say to her.

"Perhaps Brandy's just worrying because he wonders how she is."

"Perhaps if he just saw her once. . . ."

"Perhaps if she could come to tea. . . ."

They both felt that Mrs. Remnant was the one person who could really help, if they could only decide how.

When Jill got home she saw her mother standing in the hall, telephoning. If it was Auntie Katie she would ask how Brandy was behaving—she would say dreadful things if she heard what had been going on.

But it was not Auntie Katie.

"Here she is now," Jill heard her mother say. "Jill—it's Mrs. Remnant. She wants to know if Brandy has really settled down by now. What in the world am I to tell her?"

## Chapter Six

## *Blue Pink*

MRS. REMNANT was coming to tea. Jill and her mother had decided between them, in a whispered, rather frantic conversation at the telephone, that this would be best. They said nothing to Mrs. Remnant of the various disasters that had befallen, for they felt this news might upset her. They just said it would be nice to see her, and that Brandy would be pleased —and they left it at that.

"Don't you think, John," his wife said to him that evening, when he came in from work, "that it might settle Brandy to see her?"

"More likely to unsettle him."

"He's unsettled already," Jill said with a sigh.

"I knew we should get into difficulties," John said, more sad than angry. "We should never have kept him in the first place. It's all been a hideous mistake."

"But, Daddy, you know you love him!"

"When he digs holes? When he breaks pots? When he takes a nap all over my young plants? We were all much happier before he came, Jill. It's no use pretending."

"*I* wasn't happier," Jill protested. "And he's only done three awful things——"

"Four," said her mother.

"Five, Margaret. And that's not counting Donald. If he gives me his notice and moves else-where—I shall know who to blame. Brandy."

"He's lying under the table at this minute, as good as gold," cried Jill. "And I do wish you wouldn't talk about it in front of him. I'm sure he understands every word."

Saturday was the afternoon Mrs. Remnant had chosen for her visit. From the very early morning it was obvious that it was going to be nice and fine. Everyone knew that this was an important day—though quite what they all expected of it they might have found difficult to explain.

"We must make Brandy look his best, Jill," her mother said. She had already spent some time baking a special cake for Mrs. Remnant. Now she put on her special dog-grooming apron and fetched the brush and comb down from the shelf. "Brandy! Brush!"

He came at once and stood patiently while both Jill and her mother went to work on him. They brushed him till he was sleek, then combed out his

tail and the feathery parts of his legs. Then they got
an old silk scarf and gave him a final polishing. By
the time they had finished his coat was shining, it
positively glinted. He wore his beautiful studded
collar. He looked strong and splendid, a dog lovingly
cared for, properly fed, regularly exercised. He
looked, as the man in the pet shop would say, a dog
and a half.

Mrs. Remnant was due on the three-thirty bus.
Jill and Limpet went to meet her. They did not take
Brandy with them, just in case—well, in case anything happened, never mind what, to spoil the
afternoon's arrangements.

"It'll be nice to see her again, Jill," Limpet said,
as they sat side by side on the bench at the bus stop.
"Sometimes I think about her—not because of
Brandy, but because of *her*."

"Oh yes, so do I!"

"I wish she would come wearing that overall with
the flowers."

"She would never go out to tea in an overall."

"I don't want her to look like somebody else,"
Limpet objected. "Sometimes grown-ups do look
different when they're out to tea."

Suddenly they saw the bus in the distance. It was
at the top of the hill. When it got to the bottom it
would disappear, swallowed in the valley. Then it

would climb all the way up again, turn into the lane and arrive at the crossroads.

"Suppose she's forgotten? Suppose she isn't there because she's missed the bus?"

As the bus approached, they could see several people inside standing up and moving towards the door. And others were coming down the stairs, hanging on to the rail as the bus curved in to the stopping place, and the conductor shouted out the name of the village.

One by one the passengers came to the platform and stepped down. There were five, six and some more coming from above. Last came the only person of them all who did not live in the village, the only stranger. She was wearing, not a flowery overall, but a dress with a pattern of blue roses and yellow leaves.

"Mrs. Remnant! Mrs. Remnant!"

Jill and Limpet rushed towards her. They had only seen her once before in their lives, but they knew that they were running to greet a true friend.

They had tea in the garden. It was more than just tea—Mrs. Remnant somehow made it a party. Just as at their last meeting she had seemed forever on the verge of tears, so now she kept laughing. Because she had a light, soft voice, she had a tinkling laugh that sounded like a little girl's. It was the kind of laugh that made you want to join in. Even Brandy,

sitting close to her, so very close that he was nearly pushing her off her chair, seemed to have a twinkle in his usually melancholy eyes.

In fact, as time went on, it became more and more obvious that none of them there could possibly spoil Mrs. Remnant's happiness at seeing Brandy again— by telling her about holes in the lawn, smashed flower-pots or threatening growls at the nursery's newest worker.

"How beautifully you are keeping him!" Mrs. Remnant cried, fondling Brandy's ears. "I have never seen him looking better. That proves he has settled with you and is happy. No dog that was not contented could look in such excellent condition. My goodness, Brandy, you've certainly fallen on your paws!"

"He's a splendid beast," said John Hyde, avoiding the eyes of his wife and daughter. "How did you come by him in the first place?"

"My husband saw him in the window of a pet shop in London. He saw at once that the puppy looked bewildered and unhappy. He went straight in and bought him. That was eight years ago. I believe it is against the law to put puppies into shop windows nowadays. I hope so, anyway. Yes, indeed, my husband was a very gentle, kind man. Animals and flowers—those were his hobbies."

" Jill told us about your garden," Margaret said.

" I would rather not speak of it, my dear. It is all gone now. Even the ruins of the old house, which was such a fine old place once—cousins of my husband lived in it, which was why we were able to make our home there. Don't let us speak of it now. You are very fortunate here. You have the best job in the world, Mr. Hyde. I know, for my father was a nurseryman, too. Acres and acres of glass, he had. I worked with him until I married."

"Oh, then I can show you round without boring you! " cried John, delighted. "I shall show you my treasures. I am trying to breed what I tell Jill is to be a blue pink."

At this Mrs. Remnant grew so excited she almost knocked over the tea table.

"What a wonderful day this is! Wonderful! My father was the founder and president of the Downland Dianthus Society! "

Jill and Limpet looked at one another. The talk was becoming rather complicated. Jill knew that *Dianthus* was the proper name for the kind of pink her father grew, but to Limpet it sounded more like the name of some prehistoric animal.

"So you can imagine what it is like to me to be without a garden," Mrs. Remnant rushed on. "My nephew is no gardener and his wife not much better.

I am a fish out of water in that household. Though I doubt very much," she added, laughing again as though this was the biggest joke in the world, "I very much doubt if they would care to give a home to a fish!"

Very soon, they all set out on a tour of the greenhouses, Brandy with his nose close against Mrs. Remnant's dress, and Jill and Limpet trailing along behind.

As it was Saturday, there was no one working in the nursery, for they had all gone home at noon. The long glass houses, some cool, some warmly damp, were empty of all but their true inhabitants—the many thousands of plants tenderly reared and cared for by Jill's father and his staff of workers. They went through the geranium house, through houses stocked with plants whose complicated names made Limpet frown. Then they came to the carnations—rows and rows of them in small pots, neatly staked, their grey curling leaves like half-coiled springs along their sturdy stems and their fat buds bursting into reds and yellows and mauves.

At last they came to John's own particular greenhouse, where he had his treasures; among them the secret seedlings, the pinks that were meant to be blue.

Since Brandy's various offences this door had been

kept locked and the key hung on a special hook inside the kitchen door.

"There—I've left the key behind! Run and fetch it, Jill, will you?"

But before Jill had gone a yard her father called out again—

"All right—no need. The door's open."

He frowned as he spoke, wondering when he had been in there last, and how he could have been so careless as to leave the place unlocked. But since he had Mrs. Remnant with him and wanted to show her the things inside, he did not stop to worry about it now.

"Here," he said. "Here they are. They look pretty healthy, don't they? There's a promising tinge about the leaves, I think. However, I must be patient for a long while yet."

"And guard them with your life!" cried Mrs. Remnant. "I well remember my poor father being robbed of vital experiments by some scoundrel who sold them to a rival. You know my father made great progress in this very line that you have chosen." Suddenly she became extremely excited. "Mr. Hyde! I have a wonderful idea! I am so grateful to you for giving Brandy such a wonderful home—I have come to an important decision. I always said I would never part with my father's notebooks—but I am going to give them to you. Who knows, there may be some vital point in them that will help you to achieve your ambition!"

"What a wonderful offer, John!" cried his wife.

"It is indeed! How can I thank you, Mrs. Remnant?"

"Why—simply by continuing your kindness to my beautiful Brandy," she replied, beaming round at them all.

The four members of the Hyde family, not to mention Limpet, looked everywhere but at one another. If Jill had not been afraid of making her ask questions she would have flung her arms round Mrs. Remnant and hugged her. For it seemed to Jill that whatever Brandy did now, her father would just have to put up with it. He could not possibly upset Mrs. Remnant by complaining about Brandy, by asking her to take him away, or by sending him elsewhere. Her generosity made it impossible.

Jill and Limpet now clamoured to show Mrs. Remnant Little Paddock, which was Brandy's favourite place. As they walked along, feeling very well pleased with one another, Brandy started his low, grumbling growl, though he did not move from Mrs. Remnant's side.

"Hush!" she cried. "Brandy! What bad manners!"

"There's only one person he growls at, as a rule," John said. "That's Donald. He's my newest worker and he seems to me a splendid chap—but Brandy just can't like him."

At this moment Donald himself appeared from between two of the greenhouses.

"Hullo!" John said, surprised. "Why aren't you making the best of Saturday afternoon?"

"I came back with this, sir," Donald replied. He held out his hand, and on the palm was a key. "You must have put it down on the staging when you were in the greenhouse this morning—and I picked it up by mistake and put it in my own pocket. I found it when I got home and changed out of my working trousers."

"Thank you, Donald. Good of you to bring it."

"I was pretty sure you'd start worrying if you found the door open," Donald said, smiling. "Well —I'll go and get on with Saturday afternoon, then, Mr. Hyde."

"Yes, do. Thanks again."

Donald went off and John stood for a moment looking after him. Then he shrugged, tossed the key in his hand and slid it into his own pocket. "Careless of me. Remind me to lock the door on my way back. All right, old chap," he added to Brandy, who was still growling quietly, "he's gone now."

As though he had done all he could for the time being, Brandy stopped growling. Seeing where they were heading, he began to leap and run, leading Mrs. Remnant along as though he wanted to show her Little Paddock, which was his favourite place.

"You're quite right, Brandy," she told him, looking round Little Paddock with pleasure. "It's one of the prettiest little pieces of countryside I have ever seen. You lucky, lucky dog!"

Chapter Seven

# Donald

IT was time for Mrs. Remnant to say good-bye and everyone could see that she was putting it off. She did not want to leave Brandy. But it was not only that. She did not want to leave Hyde's Nursery, where everything reminded her of her young days and made her feel that her nephew's home was a poor substitute for what she had had in the past.

"Though of course they think I am much better off in a house," she told Jill and the others. "They were rather ashamed of me when I lived in a bus. But it was a wonderful, snug place. And oh the plants in the garden! It's work I miss most. Old people work well with plants, you know. I could go on for years yet."

"Oh poor Mrs. Remnant!" Margaret cried.

"I do sound ungrateful, don't I? The thing is, beggars can't be choosers—and it's so nice to choose."

"Oh, if I could have my way—since I can't get my dear old bus back—I would choose even the smallest caravan. And I would have a little garden round it, with perhaps a small greenhouse or at least a frame. And my budgerigars, and—" She broke off and was silent and everyone knew what she had been going to say. "And Brandy."

At last the visitor could no longer put off her departure. John said he would take her to the bus and all the others cried that she must come again.

Jill and Limpet were sitting close by Brandy. Limpet had an arm round his neck, and Jill was holding his collar. When Mrs. Remnant got up from her chair, they felt how Brandy tightened all his muscles, ready to jump up, too.

"Good-bye, Brandy," she said briskly, moving away from him. "Be a good boy."

When she said *Be a good boy,* Brandy undid his muscles one by one and sank down on the grass. He put his chin on his paws and watched her walk away.

Then Limpet rushed away to get an extra good dinner for Brandy, and Jill took him to Little Paddock and threw sticks for him, and after a bit he cheered up and started dashing about. Little Paddock really seemed to be his favourite place, better even than the downs. Perhaps, because it was sheltered by trees and hedges, it reminded him of the garden behind the high fence, where he had lived so happily with Mrs. Remnant.

After the tea party, Brandy seemed much more settled. It really was as though he had been worrying about Mrs. Remnant, and having seen that she was well he could now relax and get on with the business of living at Hyde's Nursery.

"He seems much younger, somehow—don't you think so, Limpet?"

"Almost like a colossal puppy," Limpet agreed.

"We shall be able to ask Mrs. Remnant to tea another time," Jill said in a satisfied voice. "I liked her even when she was sighing and crying all the time—but she was *madly* nice when she was cheerful."

They were up on the downs on a Saturday morning. They had stopped to sit on their favourite grassy hump and Brandy sat comfortably between them. They looked down, as so often before, at their two homes side by side, with Little Paddock in between. The sun glittered on the greenhouses, and in the field behind Limpet's home three cows and two sheep nibbled and tore at the grass. People went in and out

of Mr. Jeffreys' butcher shop, and Jill and Limpet had to guess who they were. Sometimes you could tell by their clothes—a red dress or a yellow skirt or a white hat.

"There's Daddy going out in the van," Jill said.

"It might be your mother."

"It isn't," cried Jill, "because there she is going out into the garden to peg some clothes on the line."

The tiny figure, in a gay pink summer dress, carried out a basket of clothes and dumped it by the

clothes-line. Jill and Limpet sat high up on their grassy hump and watched the line fill with clothes that blew out in the breeze.

"That's my petticoat. There's Daddy's green shirt. My socks—Daddy's socks—Mummy's stockings. . . ."

"Or it might be Donald," Limpet said.

"On the *line*?"

"Driving the van, silly."

Jill was silent. She sat staring down at the nursery, hoping to see the tiny figure of Donald working somewhere among the houses, so that she could prove Limpet wrong again. But there was no sign of him or anyone else. They must all have been doing inside jobs, of which there were plenty at this time of year as at any other.

"Why does Brandy hate Donald, Jill?"

"I don't like him much, either," Jill admitted. "Do you?"

Limpet shook his head. "I don't like his smile," he said in a whisper.

They sat for some time in silence. It was not only because of Brandy that Jill felt that she disliked Donald. It was something besides. He was always very cheerful, and she was forever hearing her father say how well he worked, what a useful person he was, with his enormous knowledge of plants and

their ways. Donald, John Hyde had often said, was a
wonderful find, for he knew more about the actual
science of horticulture than all the rest of them put
together.

Yet somehow he was different from the rest who
worked at the nursery. He was not kind and comfortable like the others—old Mr. Jackson, for
instance, treated all flowers and plants like people
needing loving care, and he hated having to turn any
out. Of course plants had sometimes to be thrown
away, but Jill knew her father avoided it as much as
possible, often taking time and trouble to plant un-
wanted bulbs and roots in odd corners—which was
why Little Paddock had masses of daffodils and other
spring flowers growing under the trees, and many
roses in the hedge. But it was all too easy to imagine
Donald just tearing up any plant that seemed to him
unimportant and chucking it on to the rubbish
dump.

"Also," said Limpet, nagging away at what was
most in his mind just then, "I don't see why he had
the key."

"What key?"

"The key of your father's own greenhouse—
when Mrs. Remnant came to tea."

"He said he picked it up by mistake," Jill said,
frowning.

"Jilly," said Limpet, in the low voice he saved for important matters, "suppose he's a thief."

Jill was startled by this. It was one thing to admit that you disliked a person, and quite another to say he was a thief.

"He didn't steal the key—he brought it back."

"I know he did. I don't mean that."

"Then what do you mean?" It seemed highly unlikely that they could actually know someone who would steal. "Do you mean a burglar? Do you mean he'd take the spoons and forks?"

Limpet shook his head.

"Do say what you mean!" she cried, half impatient and half excited.

Limpet's voice became so small it could hardly be heard.

"The blue pinks," he breathed.

Jill felt her heart bang with sheer fright at hearing such an idea put into words.

"Limpet! How awful! But of course—that's why Brandy. . . . Well, he's a terribly clever dog and he might be able to guess. Is that what you mean?"

Limpet nodded. He seemed unable to say another word.

"You mean that—you-know-who—was trying to take the pinks that Saturday when everyone else was out of the way—and because Mrs. Remnant was there he was disturbed?"

Again Limpet nodded vigorously.

"We must go home and warn them!" Jill cried. As usual her mind was entirely made up and she was convinced there could be no mistake.

The three of them, Brandy, Limpet, Jill, sprang up and began rushing down the hill towards home. In her excitement and alarm Jill had already forgotten how this business had started—she had forgotten that the van had gone out and her father, almost certainly, with it. She must wait for his return to warn him.

But Jill was never much good at being patient. She just could not wait. She burst into the house and poured out the story to her mother.

"Jill!" Her mother was dreadfully shocked. "That's a terrible thing to say! You must never say things like that about people—never, never!"

"But, Mummy—we're absolutely sure, Limpet and I. We're positive."

"Don't be so ridiculous. How can you be sure? You know nothing at all about it. Now I don't want to hear another word of this. You'll find yourself in serious trouble if you ever speak of it again. I mean that, Jill. It's a most cruel and wicked thing to accuse anyone of such a thing without one shred of proof. Now forget all about it. Do you understand?"

"Then why does Brandy hate him?" Jill almost shouted, made desperate by what seemed her mother's lack of understanding.

For a fraction of a second, Margaret seemed to pause. Then quickly she cried—

"Because he's a tiresome dog and for no other reason in the world. . . . You'd better go and wash your hands, then you can lay the table. It's nearly one o'clock and Daddy'll be back any moment now."

Jill opened her mouth once more, then thought better of it. She went reluctantly up the stairs. By the landing window she paused. She saw Donald just leaving the shed where he kept his bicycle during working hours. She watched him. He strode along, wheeling the bike and whistling.

And as she heard his whistle, Jill also heard another sound. Brandy was standing at the kitchen door. He was growling.

# Chapter Eight

## *News for Mrs. Remnant*

JILL knew better than to say any more about Donald. But she decided, and Limpet decided too, to keep a secret eye on him. Meanwhile Mrs. Remnant became a frequent visitor to Hyde's Nursery, where she and John discussed plant breeding by the hour.

"I wish she lived a bit nearer," John said to his wife, one day after he had taken Mrs. Remnant to the bus stop. "She's got a wonderful store of knowledge. Far more than I have."

"You're always saying people know more than you do," she replied laughing. "If it isn't Mrs. Remnant, then it's Donald."

"That reminds me," he said, "Brandy's been snarling at Donald again. That dog'll have to be kept chained up, if he doesn't behave. Are you listening, Jill?"

"He hasn't done a single bad thing for ages, Daddy. He just doesn't like Donald. I don't, either."

"But I've never seen you try to bite him."

"I could tell him. Brandy can't."

Her father chuckled and ruffled up her hair as he went by.

"You've got an answer for everything, young woman. But I don't want my best worker leaving, you know. We'll have to watch it somehow."

Jill said nothing to that. She glanced at her mother, hoping she might add a word in Brandy's defence. But although Margaret was looking a little thoughtful, she remained silent.

One day Mrs. Remnant rang up and asked if she could come to tea that afternoon. Jill and Limpet raced home from school and found her greeting Mr. and Mrs. Hyde in a very excited fashion. She was wearing a new dress and a straw hat trimmed with a pink rose. Brandy caught her mood at once. He rushed round in enormous bounding circles, tossing his heels and shaking his great head, pulling at Mrs. Remnant's skirt until she cried out in protest.

"I'm sure you have good news of some sort, Mrs. Remnant," Margaret said.

"Yes, indeed, I have. And I must tell you at once —I can't keep it to myself a moment longer. Something quite unexpected and wonderful has happened to me."

"You look as though you've been left a fortune," John told her.

"Not a fortune—but a comfortable little sum of money. It is all to do with the old house and garden. You remember the property belonged to my husband's cousin, who had completely disappeared?"

"Yes—because that was why there was a law suit about selling it for building, wasn't it?"

"I don't pretend to understand legal matters," Mrs. Remnant said cheerfully. "All I knew was that for some reason they were not able to build and I was able to stay—and then suddenly it was all changed. But now—what do you think? It seems they have at last found out about my husband's cousin, and what happened to him after he went to New Zealand. He died some years, before my husband—who was left the property over here. And so now, right out of a clear blue sky, the money paid for the ground by the building company is to come to *me*!"

She looked round at them, beaming with pleasure. They all cried out in delight at her good fortune. It was a happy and wonderful moment, for everyone saw at once that Mrs. Remnant would now be able to leave her nephew's house and have a place of her own once more.

"Of course," she ran on, "as my nephew says—and I'm afraid he's rather cross about it—if I had known the land was mine I could probably have got a fortune for it. But what do I care? I don't even want a fortune. I just want enough to be on my own again, with enough put by for a comfortable old age. So I shall find a little caravan in a place where I can have a garden—and the budgies—and that sort of thing."

"Wonderful!" John Hyde exclaimed. "Isn't it, Margaret?"

"Oh it is! We all feel so happy for you, Mrs. Remnant. And we hope that when you find somewhere to live it will be nearer to us—for it is wonderful for John to have you to talk to."

"But isn't there something we ought to discuss?" John said, glancing at Jill and Limpet, who were sitting with Brandy between them looking rather solemn.

"No, no!" cried Mrs. Remnant, understanding perfectly what he meant. "Nothing—nothing. I wouldn't do anything in the world to upset any one of you. Do remember I haven't even started to look for my new home yet. No one is to worry about anything. We are all such good friends—we must think of one another and do what is best."

Jill and Limpet sighed with relief and began to enjoy the afternoon again. Mrs. Remnant had almost ordered them not to worry. That *must* mean she would not take Brandy away from them. They

decided not to think about it any more. They began
chasing Brandy about in great excitement, and he in
his turn grew quite wild—tearing up and down,

rushing in circles, bounding here and there—until
he was obliged to go off and have a good, long drink.
Jill and Limpet left him to it and went to join the
grown-ups. They were bending over the pots in
John's own greenhouse. The "blue pinks" were

doing well. All had grown immensely, and one plant now had several tantalisingly tight buds which would not open for a long while-yet.

As usual the time went too quickly. As usual, when Mrs. Remnant sighed that she must catch her bus, John offered to drive her to the crossroads. But at that moment the telephone bell rang and he was obliged to go and deal with a business matter.

"I'll take you, then," Margaret said.

"I can quite well walk. Perhaps Jill and Limpet will come with me." She looked round. "Where's Brandy? Isn't he going to say good-bye to me today?"

"I think he's gone to sleep after all that rushing about," Limpet said.

"Don't disturb him, then. Come along. Let's go and catch my bus."

Margaret had to say good-bye rather hurriedly, for John called to her from the house where he was still telephoning—"Fetch Donald for me, my dear, will you please?"

"Do you know where he is?"

"Geraniums, I think. He knows more about this order than I do."

Just as Mrs. Remnant, with Jill and Limpet, turned out of the gate, Brandy appeared. There was nothing for it but to take him with them—which caused Jill and Limpet to exchange a rather uneasy glance.

There was only just time to catch the bus, which always got off more promptly at this time of day. As it was the rush hour, when people were coming from work and wanted to get home quickly, there were extra buses and none of them dawdled.

"Hold him!" cried Limpet suddenly.

Jill grabbed at Brandy's collar, which Limpet was already holding with both hands. The pair of them hung on as the great dog suddenly strained forward. They both knew perfectly well that if they let go he would either bound on to the bus or else follow it along the road.

Fortunately Mrs. Remnant saw nothing of this, for she had gone inside and the conductor was already collecting her fare. As the bus turned the corner and went swooping off down the hill, Brandy gradually stopped panting and tugging and stood still.

The three of them went home very slowly. Brandy made no further attempt to run away, but he seemed to plod along and Jill and Limpet both felt sure they heard him sigh more than once. They reached the gate and went in up the drive. The excitement of the afternoon had been chased away.

Suddenly Brandy stopped dead. All along his

spine the hair rose and bristled. He growled, a low furious grumble breaking into a snarl.

"Brandy—Brandy! What's the matter?"

"What's he seen, Jill?"

"Oh Limpet—something's happened!"

From among the greenhouses she heard her father's voice. He was shouting. He sounded furious. At first she could not hear what he was saying, he was shouting so. Then five words came clearly and horribly down the length of the nursery grounds:

"Nonsense! It's that infernal dog!"

## Chapter Nine

## *Rush Hour*

JILL and Limpet began to run, but Brandy was ahead of them. Suddenly the whole of the nursery seemed to be in confusion. Mr. Jackson, Mary, all the others who were just getting ready to go home, drawn by the furious voice of their employer hurried to see what was wrong.

Jill never had any doubt as to where they would find her father. She made for his own, carefully locked greenhouse. And Brandy was ahead of her with Limpet only a pace behind—making for the same spot.

"Daddy! Daddy—what's the matter?"

John swung round when he heard Jill's voice.

"*That's* what's the matter!" He pointed angrily. "What do you think of that? I knew something like this would happen sooner or later. I've been too soft-hearted, that's my worry."

Jill grabbed at Brandy's collar but he had already slid to a halt, and Limpet coming behind crashed into the pair of them.

"Oh gosh," said Limpet, in his smallest voice, staring.

The door of the greenhouse was broken in—the bottom panel was splintered into a great gaping hole. But inside it was worse. All the pots had been swept from the main shelf and lay smashed on the floor.

They were the pots of seedlings, the little plants that were intended to blossom into blue pinks and make John Hyde famous among nurserymen. There they lay, dragged out by their roots or snapped off halfway down the stem.

"Jill! Take that dog out of my sight!" her father roared.

"Wait a minute, John," his wife cried. "How could Brandy have done this? And when?"

"How? Exactly as he's done everything else destructive—with his own great strength and wickedness! When? While we were talking so cosily to Mrs. Remnant, I suppose. He was missing part of the time—you won't deny that?"

"All right. You've told me how and when. But why, John?"

"Does a dog have to have a reason for what it does?"

"He was with us when we were in here with Mrs. Remnant," Jill said. "Perhaps he got shut in—and bashed his way out when he knew she was leaving?"

"He needn't have swept all the pots down to do that!"

Jill stooped down among the ruins of the plants, picking up the broken bits tenderly.

"Here's a root. Will it grow again?"

"Yes, yes—I daresay. But this means I've wasted months and months. . . ." John suddenly became aware of everyone gathered round, gaping in horror at the ruins. "Don't all stand there staring! It's time you went home, isn't it? Then go! Jill—what did I say? Get that dog out of my sight!"

Brandy had pushed into the greenhouse, past the shattered door swinging on its hinges. Before John realised what the dog was up to, he was snuffling round inside, his nose close to the ground, snorting every other second as he came upon a scent that excited him. He chased it backwards and forwards, then followed it to the door and thrust outside again, pushing past Jill, pushing past her mother, setting off down the path, nose down, tail in the air, picking up speed as he went, like a ball rolling downhill.

"Where's he going? Brandy!"

"Oh, lét him go!"

"But what's he doing?"

"Perhaps he's picked up Mrs. Remnant's scent. . . ."

"Let him gó. A good riddance."

"Oh do let's be sensible," Margaret begged. "Don't worry, Jill. I don't suppose he'll go far."

But Jill had suddenly turned from Brandy and was looking at the battered plants she and her father between them had picked up and laid on the shelf.

"Where's the one with buds?" she cried. "It's not here! It's disappeared! Daddy—someone must have taken it!"

For a second her father just stared at the pieces in Jill's hand. Then he flung himself down and began picking over the remains on the ground, scratching among the earth and broken pots and muttering to himself as he did so.

"Well?" Margaret cried.

"She's right," he said. "Jill's right. The budded plant isn't here. It was in a marked pot, anyway, and there are no bits of that." He looked round in a stunned way. Then he stood up. "Where's Donald?" he snapped.

Mr. Jackson was still lingering, finding it altogether too difficult to leave this dramatic scene. It was he who replied—

"Gone home twenty minutes before Mrs. Hyde come calling him."

Before there could be any reply to this, before even Jill could cry out that it must be Donald, Donald who had done this awful thing, Donald who had tried to make it look like Brandy's work, Limpet tugged at her arm.

"Jill, Jill—Brandy's gone out of the gate! He's going home to Mrs. Remnant! We shall never get him back!"

"He can't get far. . . ."

"Can't he?" cried Limpet, his voice shrill and wobbling. "Can't he just! Stupid! He's gone to catch the next bus!"

Jill shouted "Come on!" and ran at once. She and Limpet tore down the path to the drive and so to the gate and out into the village street. Behind them, John Hyde was calling to his wife to telephone the police, and himself dashing towards the yellow van.

" Where does Donald live, Jackson? "

"Coppice Cottages, sir. Top o' the hill."

As Jill and Limpet turned right at the gate, John swung the van out behind them and turned left.

The extra rush-hour bus was standing at the crossroads when Brandy bounded towards it, lifting his nose from the ground for the first time. Jill and Limpet were about fifty yards behind him and so breathless they hardly knew how to take another step.

The conductor was about to ring the bell when he saw them running and very decently paused, thinking they wanted to get on the bus. What happened then was exactly what Limpet had foretold. Brandy was the one who caught the bus.

" Your dog, dear? " the conductor called to Jill. " Bit big for the rush hour, isn't he? "

"Brandy! " Jill cried, in a breathless squeak.

"Hop on, then, dear. Can't wait any longer."

"We don't want to hop on. We want Brandy to hop off."

"Hop off, Brandy," said the conductor cheerfully, giving him a shove from behind.

Brandy growled.

He was standing at the edge of the platform,

blocking the way completely. If Brandy chose, no one could get on and no one could get off.

"You've no business to bring a bad tempered dog like that on my bus," said the conductor.

"He's not bad tempered. He's just clever," cried Limpet. "Brandy, come here!"

Brandy stayed exactly where he was.

"Brandy, Brandy!" wheedled Jill.

Brandy sat down. He was panting but extremely calm. He was like a mighty rock of dogness that nobody was strong enough to shift.

Passengers who had been turning round to stare towards the scene, now rose one by one and clustered in the doorway, peering at Brandy. One or two came down from the top deck. At least three decided they could handle the situation with ease and attempted to do so. Each time, Brandy broke into a wicked snarling and bared his teeth, so that the unfortunate passengers leapt back looking very foolish.

"This has got to stop," said the conductor. He went into the bus and walked along to the driver, who slid back a little window to ask "What's up, Bert?"

When he was told, he climbed down from his seat and walked firmly along to Brandy.

"Get along out o' there!" he yelled, in the voice of a man who thinks he can handle any situation.

Brandy looked at him. He did not even bother to growl, he just lifted his lip.

A child inside the bus now started to cry. Mothers began to protest. Angry homegoers insisted that home they would go, and the conductor and the driver had better get things sorted out or there would be trouble.

"There's trouble already," said the conductor.

Jill said desperately to Limpet—"Go and get Daddy."

"But he's gone after Donald."

"Your father, then. He always knows what to do. I'll stay on the bus. Perhaps Brandy'll get off at the next stop."

Everyone seemed to think this a reasonable idea. Jill climbed on the bus and made herself as small as possible next to Brandy, and in that way the conductor was just able to shut the folding door.

It was the longest ride between two stops that Jill could remember. Everyone stared at her and seemed to think she was some sort of mad child who might behave just as fiercely as her fierce dog. How long before Limpet and his father would arrive? Mr. Jeffreys, as everyone knew, drove like the wind; so long as Limpet was able to make him realise how important this was, he might reach the next village almost as soon as the bus.

When they reached the stop, several people were waiting to get on. But as soon as the door was opened, Brandy once more settled himself across the step. The situation became exactly the same as before, except that this time there were angry people outside the bus as well as inside.

"Get the police!" someone shouted.

"Wait!" cried Jill. "Here's Mr. Jeffreys!"

Limpet's father, driving his great fast car with all the badges on the front, dashed up and stopped with a scream of tyres, within inches of the bus. Limpet and Mr. Jeffreys leapt out. Mr. Jeffreys was very cleverly brandishing an enormous bone.

"Leave it to me," he said. He was, of course, a man who knew a great deal about almost everything. He advanced, waving the bone. He drew it under Brandy's nose. Once—twice—three times. . . . At the third, Brandy's mouth began to water and he dribbled extremely. "See that?" cried Mr. Jeffreys, triumphant. "What you want at times like this is a bit of common sense."

Again he drew the bone under Brandy's nose.

"Stand back, everyone!" he commanded.

He laid the bone down in the road, about three yards away.

Brandy quivered with the effort of staying put. He

dribbled horribly. At last he heaved himself up, leapt
from the bus and grabbed the bone.

"Quick!" shouted someone.

Three people jumped off the bus, but the fourth
held back. This was understandable—for Brandy,
with the bone between his teeth, had leapt straight

back to his old place. As anyone knows, a dog with a bone is almost immovable.

"What you want at times like this," jeered one of the passengers, "is a bit of common sense."

"All right," said the bus conductor, who had been having another word with the driver, "my mate and me's decided the only thing to do. All of you waiting here must wait for the next bus. And all of you on this bus must stay where you are. This is a matter for the police—and this bus is headed straight for the police-station—non-stop." He looked at Jill as though he hated her. "Move him just two inches —if it wouldn't be too much trouble."

Jill obliged. As she did so, she shouted wildly to Limpet through the closing door—

"Get Mrs. Remnant! Tell Mummy to telephone! Her nephew's got to bring her to the police-station!"

Limpet waved and nodded vigorously and turned away at once.

The door closed, the bus moved off, its occupants by now shouting with fury and quarrelling among themselves, too. Yet all of them too frightened, or too wise, to attempt to move the dog and his bone— which he did not gnaw, but held between his paws, obviously keeping it for a moment when he had less to think about and could really enjoy it.

## Chapter Ten

## *All for the Best*

THE police-station was in a side street at the bottom of the town. It had been there a great many years. It was rather small and rather dark and the street itself was narrow and steep. There was just about room for the bus. When it drew up outside the police-station not even a pedestrian could pass.

A surprised sergeant appeared in the doorway.

"What's going on?" he asked.

The conductor, the driver and all the passengers but Jill and Brandy began to shout in answer, so that it was quite impossible for the policeman to hear what was being said. He waited for the noise to die down, then he looked at Jill and frowned.

"Haven't I seen that dog before?" he said. "Didn't he use to belong to that party living on the site there was all the fuss about—where the new flats are building?"

"*Yes!*" cried Jill, almost sobbing with relief because here at last was someone obviously sensible.

"Then what's he doing here, miss?"

"He lives with us, now, that's the thing—

because of how Mrs. Remnant had to move. But he's decided to go home, and he won't let anybody on or off the bus."

"Dear me," said the sergeant. And he glanced at the conductor and the helpless passengers, who now began to look as foolish as they had looked furious. "Draughty night they'll have of it, if we can't get him to ~~move~~."

"I think he'll move if Mrs. Remnant comes," Jill explained. "I hope somebody's telephoned her. If so, I'm sure she'll be here soon."

At this instant, three things happened all at once.

A man on the top deck suddenly scrambled down the stairs and tried to leap to freedom over Brandy's crouching body.

A small yellow van, marked Hyde's Nursery, drew up in the street behind the bus.

A large black taxi pulled up smartly ahead of the bus.

As the man jumped, Brandy sprang up. He caught the man's sleeve and pulled him down in such a way that he went into a back somersault off the bus into the arms of the sergeant.

The man was Donald.

"Hold him!" screamed Jill.

"Hold that man!" shouted John Hyde, who had leapt from the van and dashed forward.

" Brandy ! Brandy ! " Out of the taxi climbed Mrs. Remnant.

Brandy dropped Donald as the sergeant grabbed him. Mrs. Remnant rushed forward with her arms outstretched. The passengers and crew of the bus, the police, Jill, her father and mother, who was also in the van, together with Limpet and his father who now arrived to swell the crowd, all stood to watch in amazement as the fierce dog who had kept everyone at bay for so long, stood up on his hind legs and put his paws on the shoulders of the little white-haired lady who had rushed towards him. Fondly

and warmly they greeted one another on the steps of the police-station.

"Well," said the bus conductor, "if that isn't just a dog and a half then I'm not one hour late and longing for me tea."

It was nearly two hours later that Margaret Hyde cooked a bacon and egg supper for five hungry people. Mrs. Remnant took the head of the table, and they would have given Brandy the place at the other end, but he preferred to lie underneath with his nose on Mrs. Remnant's shoe. So Limpet, since he was the other guest, sat in the second best place.

"What I can't forgive Donald," said John, when they had gone over the business for the twentieth time, "is the way he tried to make it look as though Brandy was to blame."

"It was a good *mean* idea," said Limpet.

"When will you get the blue pink back?" asked Jill.

"Tomorrow, I hope. I shall go to London and fetch it."

For Donald, determined not to be caught with his plunder in his hands, had packed the plant in a parcel and posted it to an address in London, which he had confessed to the police. Once he was arrested, he made no attempt to deny what he had done—just shrugged and accepted defeat. It was the luck of the game, he had said, in an unrepentant voice.

"Now there is something we must discuss," said Mrs. Remnant. "We must discuss Brandy. He has done a good turn to Hyde's Nursery—but I can see that he has done several bad ones, too. Perhaps he is too old a dog to settle in a new home. What do you think?"

"But we love him dreadfully!" Jill cried. "Even Daddy—or he wouldn't be so mad with Donald. And Brandy doesn't *dis*-love us."

"What can we do, Jill? How can we resolve this problem?"

"For a start," said Margaret, "come and stay with us for a bit, Mrs. Remnant. I've got an idea which I haven't even discussed with John yet—so I'd better speak to him about it before I say any more."

"No—you can say what it is, my dear," John told her. "For it is probably the same as mine."

"Oh," cried Jill, "if only it is the same as mine that has just this minute grown up in my mind for the first time! Mine," she said, "is about a caravan."

"Mine, too," agreed her mother.

Her father smiled. "And about Little Paddock?" he suggested.

"Oh Daddy—yes!"

Mrs. Remnant was looking from one to the other. She was almost the Mrs. Remnant Jill and Limpet had met all those months ago when she still lived in a bus. She was blowing her nose and dabbing at her eyes and sighing. Only this time she seemed to be sighing and sniffing out of happiness.

"What do you say, Mrs. Remnant?" John asked her, "If we can get permission to put a caravan in Little Paddock—and I think we shall so long as Mr. Jeffreys agrees—"

"Oh he *will*!" cried Limpet.

"—then would you feel inclined to move in there and have a place of your own? And shall we call Brandy the rent—shared between us?"

It was some time before Mrs. Remnant could do more than nod and blow her nose and smile.

"And may I help you in the nursery?" she managed at last. "You'll be short of a worker now, and you know what I told you—the old are good with plants."

"Well, I should hope so!" he cried. "That's one of the best parts of the whole arrangement. An expert like you will make Hyde's Nursery famous one day. Why—we'll be able to work through your father's notebooks together. I can think of nothing nicer."

They all looked round the table, feeling very pleased with one another. Then Brandy, still out of sight among their feet, softly huffed, as though clearing his throat to remind them of something.

"Goodness!" cried Jill. "How awful! He's the hero—and for the first time ever we've forgotten his dinner?"

"I suppose he really *is* the hero?" John said, in his teasing voice. "After all, we shall never really know whether the scent he followed was Donald's—or Mrs. Remnant's. Perhaps we were all just lucky that Donald happened to be on that bus."

Everyone protested furiously against this.

"Anyway," Jill decided, "what does it matter? It all turned out for the best, didn't it? Quick, Limpet—run and ask your father for a wonderful hero's dinner. . . ."

But Mr. Jeffreys himself was already coming in at the door with an enormous parcel in his hands.

"Found this sirloin had got put on one side and been forgotten—ordered and never collected," he explained. "Wouldn't care to put it back in stock after it's been out of the cool for so long. Here, Brandy old boy—that's instead of a medal. Come and be a watchdog for me now and again—and I'll find you another good joint."

It was exactly the right moment for Mr. Jeffreys to arrive. Everyone smiled, for he had already, without knowing it, answered the question they wanted to put to him. If Brandy was to be his watchdog, too, then Little Paddock was the obvious place for him to live.

"He'll have three homes," Jill said. "Half for each."

"Come now, Jill—you know very well you can't have three halves of anything."

"Can't you? Can't you really?" said Jill. "Are you sure? Then—how many halves in a dog and a half?"